Dear Parents and Educators,

Welcome to Penguin Young Readers! As parents and educators, you know that each child develops at his or her own pace—in terms of speech, critical thinking, and, of course, reading. Penguin Young Readers recognizes this fact. As a result, each Penguin Young Readers book is assigned a traditional easy-to-read level (1–4) as well as a Guided Reading Level (A–P). Both of these systems will help you choose the right book for your child. Please refer to the back of each book for specific leveling information. Penguin Young Readers features esteemed authors and illustrators, stories about favorite characters, fascinating nonfiction, and more!

Llama Llama™: Llama Llama Dance Recital Fun

LEVEL **2**

GUIDED READING LEVEL **I**

This book is perfect for a **Progressing Reader** who:
- can figure out unknown words by using picture and context clues;
- can recognize beginning, middle, and ending sounds;
- can make and confirm predictions about what will happen in the text; and
- can distinguish between fiction and nonfiction.

Here are some **activities** you can do during and after reading this book:
- Make Predictions: In this story, Luna's friends help her try to feel less nervous about her dance recital. First, they have her practice in front of them. Then Llama Llama lets Luna use his dance machine. What do you think will happen at the recital?
- Sight Words: Sight words are frequently used words that readers must know just by looking at them. They are known instantly, on sight. Knowing these words helps children develop into efficient readers. As you read the story, have the child point out the sight words below.

going	her	just	over	some
had	how	know	put	then

Remember, sharing the love of reading with a child is the best gift you can give!

*Penguin Young Readers are leveled by independent reviewers applying the standards developed by Irene Fountas and Gay Su Pinnell in *Matching Books to Readers: Using Leveled Books in Guided Reading*, Heinemann, 1999.

PENGUIN YOUNG READERS
An Imprint of Penguin Random House LLC, New York

Penguin supports copyright. Copyright fuels creativity, encourages diverse voices, promotes free speech, and creates a vibrant culture. Thank you for buying an authorized edition of this book and for complying with copyright laws by not reproducing, scanning, or distributing any part of it in any form without permission. You are supporting writers and allowing Penguin to continue to publish books for every reader.

The publisher does not have any control over and does not assume any responsibility for author or third-party websites or their content.

Copyright © Anna E. Dewdney Literary Trust. Copyright © 2019 Genius Brands International, Inc. Published by Penguin Young Readers, an imprint of Penguin Random House LLC, New York. Manufactured in China.

Visit us online at www.penguinrandomhouse.com.

ISBN 9780593092910 (pbk)   10 9 8 7 6 5 4 3 2 1
ISBN 9780593092927 (hc)   10 9 8 7 6 5 4 3 2 1

PENGUIN YOUNG READERS

LEVEL

PROGRESSING
READER

2

llama llama™
dance recital fun

based on the bestselling children's book series
by Anna Dewdney

Llama Llama is happy.

He is watching Luna

Giraffe practice her

dance steps.

"That was great!"

Llama Llama says.

Luna has a recital soon.

She feels nervous.

"I have a tummy ache!"

Luna says.

Llama Llama and Nelly Gnu try
to help Luna.

"I know you will be great, Luna,"
says Llama Llama.

But Luna is still nervous.

She needs fresh air

to calm down.

Llama Llama has an idea.

"You can practice for us!"

he says.

"I'll try," says Luna.

Luna puts on some music

to practice.

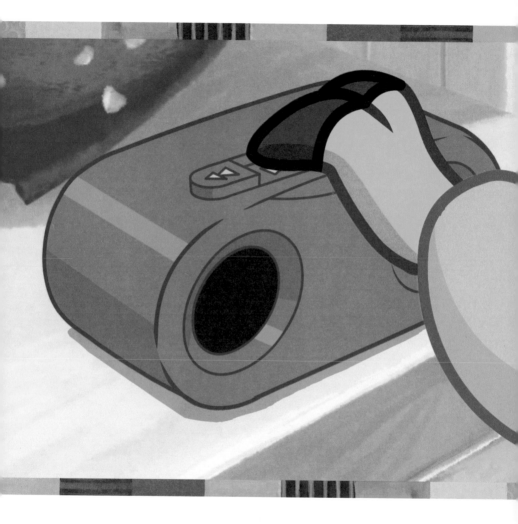

Oh no!

She still feels nervous.

Llama Llama knows how to help Luna.

He invites her over to his house to play.

He has a surprise for Luna.

"It's a dance machine!"

says Llama Llama.

Mama Llama tells Luna that it is just for fun.

"A few deep breaths help me feel calmer," says Mama Llama.

Luna takes some deep breaths.

Now she is calm and having fun.

"Go, Luna!" calls Nelly Gnu.

The next day, everyone gathers for the dance recital.

"I hope Luna is not so nervous anymore," says Llama Llama.

"You and Nelly are such good friends for trying to help her," says Mama Llama.

"I'm sure she's going to be fine," she says.

"Welcome to our dance recital!"

says Zelda Zebra.

The dancers begin to perform.

Oh no!
Luna is missing.
Llama Llama and
Nelly Gnu help look
for her.

Nelly Gnu searches the

school halls.

Llama Llama searches

the classrooms.

"Luna, where are you?"

asks Llama Llama.

There she is!

Luna is outside.

22

Luna is still too nervous to perform onstage.

"I can't dance with everyone watching me," she says.

Llama Llama helps Luna.

"We're excited to see you dance,"

Llama Llama says.

Luna takes a few deep breaths.

"I'm going to try," Luna says.

"The show must go on!"

The friends race back inside.

Nelly Gnu reminds Luna
how much fun they had
on the dance machine.

"Just dance and try to have fun,"

says Llama Llama.

Llama Llama has an idea!

He brings the dance machine

to the stage.

"Put your hands together for

Luna Giraffe and Friends!"

First, Llama Llama dances onstage.

Then more friends come up to dance!

Now it is Luna's turn.

She takes a deep breath and

dances perfectly!

Everyone cheers.

Luna is so happy.

She is lucky to have

such great friends.

Mama Llama is proud of
Llama Llama for helping Luna.
They celebrate in the best
possible way—
with ice cream and
a dance party!